snot, snails and salamander tails

by **Ann Campbell**

illustrated by **Marianne Harris**

Just Enjoy!
Ann Campbell

Love
The
Felts

◆ FriesenPress

Suite 300 - 990 Fort St
Victoria, BC, V8V 3K2
Canada

www.friesenpress.com

ISBN
978-1-5255-0630-7 (Paperback)
978-1-5255-0631-4 (eBook)

1. JUVENILE FICTION, READERS, BEGINNER

Distributed to the trade by The Ingram Book Company

Dedication

This story is dedicated to our youngest granddaughter, Bronwyn Campbell, affectionately known as "B". Her Dad's favorite story, *The Three Billy Goats Gruff*, was the inspiration for me to write this spin-off on the old tale.

"SNOT, SNAILS AND SALAMANDER TAILS"

Tappity tap, tappity tap, went little Gustaff Gruff on the bridge with his hooves.

"Stop **that tapping!"** shouted the troll. "I have a runny nose and a terrible headache."

"I was just practicing my dance before my lesson with Grandpa Gruff," said little Gustaff. "Would you like to come along? Grandpa will know how to make you feel better."

"No, I have to stay and stir my stew," replied the troll, "but it's a terrible stew and a yucky thing to do."

"**What's** in it that makes it so terrible?" asked little Gustaff.

"Snot, snails and salamander tails,"

said the troll, "but
I'd love to catch
something tasty like

YOU,"

so he tried to catch the little goat by the tail, but all
he caught were a few hairs.

"**YOU** should wait for my bigger brother," called the little goat. "He would make more stew than I would," so the troll stayed behind to stir his stew, but just as he took a sniff, his nose went

drip, drip,

drip.

Soon Gordon Gruff began to practice his dance,

tappity tap,
tappity tap,

on the bridge.

"Stop  that tapping!"

yelled the troll. "I have a runny nose and your tapping sounds like hammers in my head."

"But this bridge is the best place to practice my dance before my lesson with Grandpa Gruff," said Gordon. "Would you like to come along? Grandpa will know how to make you feel better."

"NO, I have to stay and stir my stew," replied the troll. "It's a terrible stew, and a yucky thing to do, but it wouldn't be terrible if I could catch YOU," so he tried to grab Gordon by the hoof, but the goat kicked and got away.

"Try catching my biggest brother," called Gordon. "He has big horns to go in your stew,"

SO the troll stayed behind to stir his stew, but just as he took a sniff, his nose went drip, drip,

drip,

drip.

Soon Griswold Gruff began to practice his dance,

tappity tap, tappity tap, on the bridge.

"Stop that tapping!"

roared the troll. "I have a runny nose, and your tapping sounds like thunder in my head. I suppose you're also going to your Grandpa's for a lesson."

"I am," said Griswold. "You should come along, but bring your pyjamas. We're having a sleepover."

"No, I have to stay and stir my stew," replied the Troll. "It's such a terrible stew, and a yucky thing to do, but it wouldn't be terrible if I could catch YOU," so he tried to catch Griswold by the horns, but the goat sent him flying off the bridge.

"Try catching Grandpa Gruff," called Griswold. "He's coming back with us tomorrow and has a long stringy beard for your stew,"

SO the troll stayed behind to stir his stew, but just as he took a sniff, his nose went

drip drip, drip, drip.

Hmmm, I must catch them tomorrow, thought the troll, so he came up with a plan to trick them off the bridge and into the pot.

"**Please** join me for Snot Stew!" said the troll as the goats came onto the bridge.

Eeeew, thought the goats, but to be polite, they ate it anyway.

They were ready to leave when the troll said, "You should show me your dances here on the bridge. Who wants to go first?"

"Not I," said Griswold. "I've been dancing a lot. I'm too tired."

"Not I," said Gordon. "I ate a big bowl of stew. I'm too full."

"Not I," said little Gustaff. "I might dance too close to the edge. I'm too afraid."

"I will dance," said Grandpa to the troll, "but not alone. If you join me on the bridge, I'll teach you a dance."

Aha, thought the troll. *Now I can push the old goat off the bridge and into the pot of stew.*

"Tap with your right toe, and tap with your left," said Grandpa Gruff.

"Then take two steps toward the edge of the bridge, and do that over and over."

The troll did as Grandpa said, right into the pot of stew!

"YUK!" said the troll, as he climbed out of the pot. "You should come for stew again tomorrow, but teach me a different dance. I don't like that one."

"No thanks," said Grandpa Gruff.

"We're inviting you for stew tomorrow."

The next day, the goats gathered all the farmer's stinky socks from the trash heap and made a big pot of stew.

"**Welcome**," they said.
"Please join us for Stinky Sock Stew."

"Stinky Sock Stew!" cried the troll,
and he took a tiny sip.

"Eeeeeeeew!

My stew is better than that!" he
shouted as he ran home.

In the morning, Grandpa Gruff and the goats returned to the bridge.

"That's a terrible stew!" said Griswold.

"And yucky too!"

said Gordon.

"I wish he could find something new for his stew," said little Gustaff.

"I think he just did," said Grandpa Gruff, looking back.

"Mmmmmm," said the troll, as he dropped his own stinky socks into the stew. "These will be better than snot, snails and salamander tails."

"I agree," said the snail and the salamander wagged his tail, but just as the troll took a sniff, his nose went

drip drip, drip

CPSIA information can be obtained
at www.ICGtesting.com
Printed in the USA
LVOW06s2215050517

533454LV00005B/5/P

9 781525 506307